LEVEL UP!

UP!

BLOCK AND ROLL

D0248118

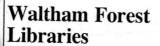

STRIPES PUBLISHING LIMITED
An imprint of the Little Tiger Group
1 Coda Studios, 189 Munster Road,
London SW6 6AW

A paperback original
First published in Great Britain in 2019

Text copyright © Tom Nicoll, 2019
Illustrations copyright © Anjan Sarkar, 2019

ISBN: 978-1-78895-075-6

TOM NICOLL

LEVEL UP!

BLOCK AND ROLL

ILLUSTRATED BY

ANJAN SARKAR

Stripes

LEVEL 1

"ARRRRRRGHHHHHHHHH!"

If you've ever woken up inside a strange cabin with
your best friend and immediately answered the
door to reveal a tentacled monster made entirely
from bright green bricks, then you'll know exactly
what Max and I were going through. If not, well …
I wouldn't recommend it.

I did the only sensible
thing you can do in such a
situation and slammed
the door shut.

"What the heck was that?" I asked.

"It was like … a person crossed with an octopus," said Max slowly. "Only made from bricks. Just like we're made from bricks and this room is made from bricks. And I only caught a glimpse of outside, but everything out there looks like it's made from bricks too! You realize what this means?"

"Does it have something to do with bricks?" I asked.

"We're in another game," he said.

Another game? "So that means…" I said, taking a large breath. "Mum's machine did transport us into a video game and we really did fly a spaceship, defeat the Red Ghost and convince an army of Space Soldiers to follow their dreams, which we hoped would let us leave the game but instead we've teleported to another game where everything's made from bricks and there's a monster outside?"

Max nodded. "Yeah, sounds about right," he said.

"OK," I said. "Just checking. Mum was right about us leaving the game once we completed it, but she didn't say anything about jumping right into another one. What is this anyway?"

Max looked stunned. "Seriously? You're the biggest gamer I've ever met and you don't recognize this one?"

"No… Oh, wait, hang on," I said, the penny dropping. "Tell me it's not that boring one where you just have to mine and build stuff?"

"*Blocktopia* isn't boring!" protested Max. "It's the only video game I've ever been interested in."

I nodded. "That's what I said – it's boring."

Max scowled at me. "Just because you don't have to shoot everything in sight doesn't make it boring," he said. "*Blocktopia* lets you build an entire world exactly how you want it to be. It's amazing."

I shrugged. "Whatever you say," I replied. "There's still the tentacled person outside to deal with."

"That's an Octoperson," said Max. "One of the monsters you get in the game."

"Friendly?" I asked hopefully.

Max shook his head. "Not in the slightest."

"Pity," I said. "So how do we stop them? What's your weak point if you've got eight arms?"

"Finding clothes that fit?" asked Max.

Rolling my eyes at his bad joke, I pressed my ear to the door. "I don't hear anything. Maybe it's gone?"

Knock-knock.

"Maybe not," I said, leaping back.

"Hello?" shouted a voice from outside. "Is anyone in there? I can see your light on."

The voice sounded human, but then maybe Octopeople could speak. I looked at Max for a clue.

"I think it's someone else," he said.

I pushed open the door. Standing outside this time were three Block People, one short and two not-so-short, dressed in blue uniforms with golden badges on them, carrying torches and pitchforks.

"Who are you?" I asked.

"We're City Guards," said the smallest of the three. "They call me Stoneheart 'cos that's my name. But more to the point, who are you two? And what are you doing here?"

"I'm Flo and this is Max, and um…" I said, trying to think how best to answer the second question.

"Never mind, that can wait," said Stoneheart, cutting me off. "An Octoperson was spotted nearby. Did either of you see it?"

"It was here a minute ago," Max answered. "But we shut the door on it."

"So you didn't see where it went?" he asked.

We shook our heads. Stoneheart frowned. "We must have just missed it. It can't have gone far." He turned to the other two Block People. "Sweep the perimeter, then go from house to house."

They scampered off and Stoneheart turned his attention back to us.

"You two are coming with me," he said.

"Coming with you where?" I said.

"To the Architect," he replied. "He'll know what to do with you."

LEVEL 2

We were led outside and into what I supposed was meant to be a car. But in a world where everything was made from bricks some things worked better than others.

"S-s-sorry f-f-for th-th-the b-b-bumpy r-r-ride," said Stoneheart.

"D-d-do y-y-you r-r-really th-th-think c-c-cubes a-a-re th-th-the b-b-best sh-sh-shape f-f-for wh-wh-wheels?" I asked, as we bounced along the road.

"Wh-wh-what o-o-other o-o-ones a-a-are th-the-there?" he laughed.

I had no reply. How do you explain different shapes to someone in a world where there's only one? Instead I looked out of the window and observed the strange city around us. Dawn was starting to break and rays of early morning light cut through the neatly ordered rows of identical wooden houses. Max had always described *Blocktopia* as endlessly creative, but I couldn't help noticing how similar everything was. Every house was the same as the last. Until we came to one that wasn't.

We'd left the other houses behind, travelling down a long driveway in what looked like a country estate, with acres of green grass, tall trees and a couple of blue lakes surrounding a huge mansion that made Max's eyes light up.

"Now that's what I call a house," he said, as the car pulled up in front of it.

"Look at the size of it," I agreed, stepping out on to a gravel path.

"The home of the Architect," said Stoneheart.

We followed him inside and up a winding staircase. "He's a big deal, then, this Architect?" I asked.

"The biggest," he replied. "Our people owe him everything. He's a genius. A visionary. Our guiding light."

"Stoneheart, you flatter me," came a voice. We looked up to see a man waiting for us at the top of the stairs. He had black hair and a goatee beard and wore a red velvet jacket with black trousers and a little square beret on his head.

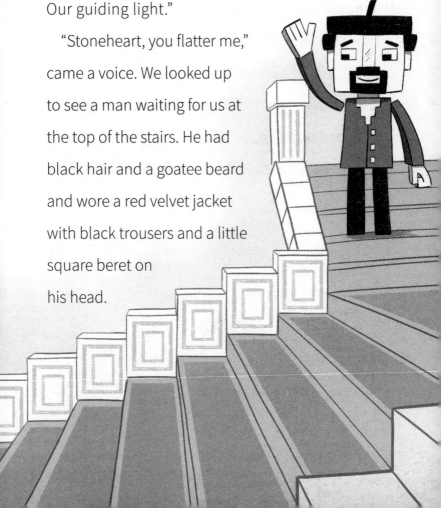

"Sir, apologies, I didn't see you there," said Stoneheart, climbing the last few steps.

"No need to apologize, Stoneheart," he said. "And I've told you before, please don't call me sir. My name is Carl."

"Yes, sir," said Stoneheart. "Sorry, sir."

"Who have you brought here?" said Carl, looking us over. "Friends, I hope?"

"Still to be decided," said Stoneheart. "Me and a couple of the guards were out investigating reports of Octopeople on the outskirts of the city. No sign of them, but we came across these two hiding out in one of the older cabins."

"I see," Carl responded. "Do they have names?"

"One's called Flo, the other's Max," said Stoneheart.

"And what exactly were you two doing out

there?" asked Carl.

Max and I looked at each other. "Hiding from the tentacle person," I said, which seemed like the closest thing to a true answer that he'd understand.

He said nothing for a few seconds then laughed. "Oh, you mean the Octopeople?" he said. "Of course you were! Always been trouble, that lot. Cause us no end of bother, destroying our buildings, stealing our resources, upsetting our people. You two must have been terrified."

We both shrugged. "At first," I admitted. "But it didn't really do anything. It just knocked on the door."

"It would have done more than that if my men and I hadn't shown up," interjected Stoneheart.

"Oh, undeniably," agreed Carl. "Stoneheart, would you mind waiting outside?"

Stoneheart looked confused. "You want me to leave you alone with them?"

"I don't think they plan on harming me, if that's what you're worried about," said Carl. He turned to us. "You don't, do you?"

"No," we said together.

"There now, you see." Carl laughed. "I've always been a good judge of character."

"As you wish, sir," said Stoneheart, before taking his leave.

"Please, join me in my office," Carl said, leading us down a corridor and into a room with a huge desk in front of two large windows. The sun was fully up now and from where we stood you could see beyond the grounds to the city. I had to admit it was an impressive sight.

"Beautiful, isn't it?" said Carl.

"It's really something," said Max. "What it's called?"

"We call it Sublimity," he replied, sitting behind the desk. "It took a very long time to build. Of course, if you were to ask the people, they'd say I'm the one to thank for it. And yes, while it's true that I designed everything in the city, from the tiniest toilet to the biggest ballroom, I simply can't take all the credit. It was the people who took my ideas and turned them into reality. Do you know what the secret to the perfect city is?"

Max and I gave this some thought.

"Good Wi-Fi?" I asked.

"Donuts?" said Max.

"Donuts?" I repeated.

"I don't know, I panicked!" said Max.

Carl looked puzzled. "I don't know what those

things are but no, not them. The secret to a perfect city is the people who live in it."

"*People*. I should have said that," Max muttered under his breath.

"My question to you two, then, is this," said Carl. "What kind of people are you?"

It felt like a test, but one where I wasn't really sure what the question was. "Um … the good kind?" I said.

Carl nodded. "Are you the kind willing to contribute to the greater good?" he asked. "Because that's the kind of people we need in Sublimity. We're making something special here. A city like no other. The *perfect* city. We could always use more hands to build it."

It took me a moment to realize he was offering us a job. "Thanks for the offer," I said, "but Max and I need to get home."

My rejection seemed to catch Carl off guard. "Home?" he said, sounding a little irritated. "Where is that?"

"You wouldn't know it," I said.

Max reached for my arm. "Carl, sorry, would you mind if I spoke to Flo in private?"

"Of course," said Carl.

Max pulled me over to the far corner of the room.

"You're not actually considering we take him up on his offer? We need to get home!" I said.

"And how are we going to do that?" asked Max.

 "Well, obviously we'll…" I began, my voice trailing off as I realized I hadn't thought that far ahead. Then, like a flash of lightning, it hit me. "Mum! She helped us last time by joining the

game in the real world. She'll do the same again. We just need to wait for her…" Something else occurred to me. "Oh no," I said quietly.

"Oh no what?" said Max nervously.

"*Blocktopia* is one of those annoying games that makes you sign into a special account just for that game," I said. "Even if you're already logged into your *G-Locker* account."

Video Game Tip: G-Locker is an app that stores all your games in one handy place, which is brilliant. Unless it ever stops working, in which case you lose every game you own. It's probably best not to think too much about that.

"Let me guess," said Max. "Your mum doesn't know your *Blocktopia* password?"

"I don't even know it," I said. "I only played this game once after you convinced me to buy it. Most boring game ever."

Max sighed. "That settles it then. We have to help build the city."

"Why?" I asked.

"Because," said Max, "in *Star Smasher*, we had to complete the game to leave it, right?"

I nodded. It was dawning on me where he was going with this.

"There's only one way to complete *Blocktopia*," he said. "And that's to build the perfect city."

I let out a moan. "But I hate building games."

"I hate space battles but you didn't hear me complaining last time," Max said.

"Pretty sure that's not true," I shot back.

Max grinned. "Hey, Carl!" he shouted. "Count us in."

"Wonderful," said Carl. "Then let's begin."

LEVEL 3

"This isn't what I expected." Max sighed.

"Serves you right," I muttered.

We were gathered in front of several damaged cottages. Most of them had huge holes in their front wall, like someone had tried opening the door with a tank shell. Carl had informed us that these were recent casualties of raids from a group of monsters known as Boulder People. It was our job to fix the mess they'd left behind.

"Here's the Tutorials," said a small, stubbly man wearing a hard hat and a high-visibility vest, handing Max a thick red book. The man was called Brick and he was the site foreman. Carl had left us with him and he seemed to think he was in charge.

"The Tutorials?" I asked.

"Everything you could ever need to know about building stuff is in there," said Brick. He thumbed to

a page with a diagram of a cottage identical to the ones around us, except without random bits missing. "This is the only thing you'll need today, though."

Max looked over the instructions. "Is that all you want us to do?" he asked. "You know, I have quite a lot of experience at this game."

"Game?" said Brick, screwing up his face.

"He means the house-building game," I said, covering his slip.

"Er... Yeah, the old house-building game," said Max. "Anyway, I could make some real improvements to these cottages if you want."

Brick stared at us like we'd just stolen his breakfast. "The only improvements these houses need are new doors," he said.

Max wasn't put off. "What if we gave them another level or two?" he asked. "Turn them from bungalows into townhouses? Or what if we—"

"No!" snapped Brick. "Just stick to the plans. We're builders. We build. We already have an architect, and I think he knows more than either of you about how to build houses. So just follow the instructions, OK?"

Max and I nodded.

"Good. Any more questions?" he asked. "Or can I go and have my breakfast now?"

Max slowly raised his hand. Brick sighed. "What?"

"Where do we get blocks to build with?" he asked.

Brick grinned. "Ah, yeah, right enough." He put his fingers to his mouth and made a piercing whistle. A few moments later a younger builder appeared carrying a small chest. He dumped it at our feet then scurried off again.

"Everything you need is in there," said Brick. "I'll be back in a bit to see how you're getting on."

After Brick left, I turned to Max shaking my head. "Is he having a laugh?" I said, pointing at the chest. "Look at that thing. It's so small! We're going to need loads of blocks to fix these houses. You'd be lucky to fit one block in there."

Max just smiled annoyingly and opened the chest. Inside was an assortment of different-coloured blocks, neatly stored in individual containers. There was still an obvious issue, though.

"They're tiny," I said.

"Watch," said Max, taking out a little brown cube. He held it in his palm for a second before the tiny block seemed to dissolve into his hand.

"Whoa," I said.

Max snapped his fingers in the air in front of us and a large block of wood appeared. A few more snaps and he'd laid out a timber porch.

"Cool," I said.

"Each of these tiny blocks gives you the ability to lay twenty regular-size blocks," explained Max. "They're handy to have, otherwise you need to mine for individual blocks, and we don't have the tools for that."

"I want a go," I said, reaching into the chest. I took out a red brick and watched as it melted into my hand. I pointed towards the patch of grass in front of me.

"FLO, NO!" yelled Max, as he tackled me to the ground.

"What are you—" Before I could finish speaking there was a flash of red light. In the space where I'd just been standing a small crater appeared.

"That was a firebrick," said Max. "It's an explosive."

"Yeah, I noticed," I said, as we got to our feet.

"Hey, what's going on?" shouted Brick, peeking
out from behind a house several blocks down.

"Nothing," Max yelled back. "Just an accident."

Brick shook his head and disappeared.

Max pointed at a few different brick types in the
chest. "Let's just stick to these ones," he said. He
quickly filled in the hole in the ground and then we
got to work.

I was so bored. In fact, I hadn't been as bored as
this since the time Mum banned me from playing
video games for an entire weekend. We'd been

fixing houses for hours. Maybe even years. And we'd done millions of houses. It had been so long, and so many, that I had lost count. I asked Max if he remembered.

"It's been half an hour," he said. "And we've fixed three houses."

"What?" I exclaimed. "That can't be right."

"Well, no," admitted Max. "I should have said *I've* fixed three houses. You've just sat around and complained."

"Glad to help," I said. "I thought you told me this game was all about building whatever you wanted?"

"It is," said Max. "Normally, anyway."

"This is *DIY: the video game*," I said. I looked up and down the street but couldn't see any sign of Brick or the other builders. "There's no one about. Let's have some fun and actually build something!"

Max groaned. "Flo, come on," he said. "Let's stick to the plan."

I'd known Max a long time and I could tell that despite what he was saying, he was bored too. I knew he wanted to build something of his own. All he needed was someone to get the ball rolling. That someone was me. I started slapping down bricks on to the roof.

"What are you doing?" asked Max.

"I'm giving it a second level," I said. "Like you suggested."

Max frowned. "Yeah, but not like that," he said. "Let me show you."

I stood back, grinning, as Max eagerly set to work extending the building. In a short time we'd created a masterpiece. And I do mean 'we' this time. By the time we were done, the house had five levels. Max had worked on the inside, building eight bedrooms, seven bathrooms, a kitchen, a dining room, a living room and a games room. Then he knocked holes in every one of them and connected them with a gigantic indoor roller coaster. I had focused on the outside, giving the house giant arms and legs and several rocket launchers.

"It's magnificent," I said, as we admired our handiwork.

"Still not completely sure about the arms, legs and rocket launchers," said Max. "But yeah, it's pretty cool. I've got loads of ideas for the next one..."

"What's this?"

We spun round to see Carl, followed closely by Stoneheart, Brick and several builders. They all looked horrified, apart from Carl whose face gave nothing away.

"Oh, hi, Carl," said Max. "We were just playing around. What do you think?"

Carl looked up at the house, evidently giving the question some thought.

"I love it!" he said. "What wonderful imaginations you both have."

Max and I grinned at each other.

"It's a shame that it'll have to come down," said Carl.

"Come down?" I said. "But why? You just said you loved it."

"Oh, I do," said Carl. "But … you remember when I talked about the greater good? Unfortunately, sometimes doing things for the greater good requires making difficult decisions. While it would be delightful to live in a city where we can build anything we want, there are other issues to consider. Like resources. The amount of materials you put into building your fantastic house could have been used to build five or six houses. And resources aren't endless, you know."

"We hadn't thought about that," admitted Max.

"Not to mention that if we build one house like that, other people are going to want them too," he continued. "These are the kinds of problems that I, as the Architect, have spent my entire life trying to solve. It's what led me to creating the Tutorials. Only by following the instructions can we create the perfect city."

Max nodded. "We understand," he said. "Right, Flo?"

I shrugged. It all seemed a bit over the top to me. I still thought our house was amazing but I could tell from Max's face that he wanted to play along.

"Right," I said. "We'll stick to the plan next time."

Carl smiled. "Thank you," he said. "You know what, after seeing what you two can do, I think your talents might be wasted here."

"You do?" asked Max, his face lighting up.

"I do," said Carl. "I have a project that I think would suit you better. With all these raids our city has been suffering, we've been doubling our efforts on the last stage of making Sublimity truly perfect. We're building a wall round the city that will finally make us safe. It will be the greatest structure ever created and I think you two have got just what we need to help us complete it sooner."

"Brilliant," said Max. "A promotion!"

But it wasn't. Not even close.

LEVEL 4

"This has to be some kind of mistake," protested Max.

"Are you Max and Flo?" asked the older man with a grey block-beard.

"Yes, but—" said Max.

"Then there's no mistake," he said, handing us each an iron pickaxe. "You'll be needing these. That's your section over there. You take the pickaxe, you break the blocks, you get the materials. Simple as that. Remember, we need iron, gold and stone for the wall, so don't be wasting my time bringing me coal or some other nonsense."

Video Game Tip: Some blocks, like dirt and sand, can be smashed by hand, but you'll need a good pickaxe for most other types, especially if you want to extract resources from blocks.

"They call me Digger, by the way," he added.

First Brick the builder and now Digger the miner. Max and I left him to it and made our way over to the corner of the mine. It was dark and dingy as I guessed mines tended to be. Here and there other miners were busy, either breaking blocks or handing over the materials to Digger. A few lanterns had been placed throughout the chamber, but they only provided just enough light to make out the look of annoyance on Max's face.

"I can't believe this," he moaned.

"Not what you were expecting, huh?" I said.

"No," said Max. "I should never have listened to you! If I was building that wall I'd have it done in no time. I'd have completed their perfect city and then we might have been able to go home sooner. I mean, we're still helping – mining is an important part of the game – but it's not exactly the best use of my skills. We should have just stuck to Carl's designs."

"Carl's super-boring designs," I corrected.

"They were boring," admitted Max. "But they weren't as boring as this."

He was right. As dull as the house maintenance had been, this was worse. We spent the next few hours smashing bricks with our pickaxes, collecting different block types and giving them to Digger. Over and over again. It wasn't tiring – tiredness isn't a thing in *Blocktopia* apparently – but it was most definitely tiresome.

"It *has* been hours this time, right?" I asked Max.

"At least," said Max distractedly, as he turned a page in the Tutorials.

Max and I hadn't really spoken for most of our time in the cave. I think he was still annoyed with me, since it had been my idea to make changes to the house. But I hadn't made him build those extra four floors. I'd have been fine with just adding rocket launchers.

I was about to say as much when a siren went off and flashing red lights began reflecting on the walls of the cave.

"What's going on?" I shouted over the noise.

"Everyone out!" yelled Digger.

Max and I did what we were told, following Digger and the other miners out of the cave. It was nighttime now, confirming that we had been in the mines for more than a few hours. Outside, it was chaos. People were running everywhere, screaming as bells rang and sirens blared. It still wasn't clear why.

"It's another raid," said Digger.

A group of people ran past us, carrying pitchforks, burning torches and other makeshift weapons.

Digger grabbed a woman's arm. "Who is it this time?" he asked.

"Boulder People," she said.

"Oh, man, they're the worst," groaned Digger.

"The guards pushed most of them back, but there are still some left," she said, before rushing off.

Digger turned to us and the rest of the miners. "All right, crew, everyone armed? Good. Let's go and give them a hand."

Max and I were almost carried along by the rest of the miners as they hurried through the streets waving their pickaxes above their heads. In several of the houses we passed there were obvious signs of damage. Entire doorways were missing and blocks were scattered around the street.

It was Max who saw it first.

"Look!" he shouted, pointing towards what looked like a supermarket across the road from us. A giant grey figure was trying to squeeze itself through the entrance. It was about twice the size of a Block Person and seemed to be made entirely from concrete.

Several of the miners began to approach the Boulder Person, their pickaxes ready to strike. Their footsteps must have given them away, though, as the Boulder Person spun round, ripping out half of the storefront in the process. It gave a deafening roar, which was enough to make a couple of the miners run screaming into the night. As for those who stuck around, the Boulder Person flung several huge stone blocks towards them.

The miners protected themselves by smashing the blocks in mid-air with their pickaxes. Some of them retreated back to our position, but more fled down the street. There were around twenty of us left, but it was clear we were outmatched.

"What should we do?" I asked Digger.

"I … I … don't know," he said. "I thought with our pickaxes our numbers would be enough but what do I know – I'm a miner not a fighter."

I turned to Max, hoping he might be more use. But he wasn't there.

"Max!" I shouted, looking around.

"There!" said Digger, pointing at the supermarket. Sprinting towards the Boulder Person was Max.

"Max, what are you doing?" I yelled.

Max didn't reply as the Boulder Person roared before launching another volley of blocks at him. Max didn't bother using his pickaxe, instead diving out of the way as he continued to cut the distance between himself and the monster. When he was only a few metres away, Max launched his own attack. And by attack, I mean he started building.

It was a blur. Blocks seemed to fall at random, only they weren't random. All the while Max was bouncing here, there and everywhere. One second he was in front of the Boulder Person, the next he was behind it. As the Boulder Person swung out at Max, the blocks continued to fall around it, stacking up until we couldn't see it any more. Max had encased it in a small prison.

A cheer went up among the miners.

"That's incredible," said Digger, as we all crowded round Max. "I've never seen building like that."

"It was kind of cool," I admitted. "But that thing looked pretty strong. Won't it just be able to smash its way out of there?"

Max opened his mouth to speak, but another voice answered instead. "No, it won't," said Carl, standing behind us with Stoneheart and several other guards. "Because that's a Class 3 iron-enforced holding cell. Impenetrable even by the Boulder People."

"Straight from the Tutorials," said Max.

"Indeed," said Carl, visibly impressed.

"He built it in ten seconds," said Digger.

"Hmm," said Carl, stroking his goatee. "Perhaps mining isn't the best use of your talents after all.

I think a transfer to the Great Wall team would be a wise move."

"Thanks, Carl!" said Max, seeming a lot happier. I had to admit the thought of not going back to the mine was pretty nice.

"Here's your pickaxe back, then," I said, offering it to Digger. But instead of taking it, Digger looked away nervously. A weird silence filled the air. Max was staring at the ground and Carl had a pained expression on his face.

"HUR-HUR!" boomed the Boulder Person from within its cell. "He doesn't mean you, little girl. He just means the boy. How awkward, hur-hur!"

LEVEL 5

"Are you serious?" I asked, looking at Carl. "You want me to go back to the mines, without Max?"

"Building the perfect city requires knowing where best to allocate resources," said Carl. "As Architect, I need to be practical. We need people mining and we need people building. If this night has taught us anything it's that we must get that wall up as fast as we can."

"We'll stick to mining then, right, Max?" I said.

Max didn't reply.

"*Right*, Max?" I repeated, more assertively.

"Flo, it's just I think Carl might be right," he said.

If it had been awkward before, this was something else. I could feel my face reddening. "Fine," I snapped. "Enjoy building your stupid wall, then."

"The wall *is* stupid," agreed the Boulder Person.

"Shut up," I said, as I stormed off.

"Flo … are you all right?" asked Digger.

"Fine," I said, as I swung my pickaxe back before bringing it crashing down on a black block, earning myself a lump of coal.

"Don't you think you should probably take a break now?" he said. "You've been going at it for hours."

"We need resources, don't we?" I asked, swinging again. Iron this time. Better.

"Yes … but…" said Digger.

"Then I'll get you resources," I said, raising my
pickaxe again. This time Digger grabbed hold of it.

"Flo, come on," he said. "You've personally mined
more blocks in the last few hours than the rest of
my crew has in the last week. To be honest, you're
making us look bad. As your boss, I'm ordering

51

you to take a break. Go outside, get some fresh air, stretch your legs a bit."

I tried to pull my pickaxe free but Digger wasn't having it. "Why don't you take this instead?" he offered, handing me a piece of paper. "It's a map of the city. Go see some of the sights. There's the Museum of Natural Blocks, that's a good one. Or City Square. You'll need the map to find that since, you know, everywhere is square. It's the really big one in the middle."

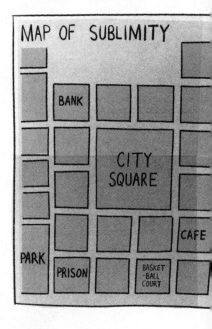

"OK," I said, letting go of the pickaxe and snatching the map. I stuffed it into my pocket and marched outside, the light almost blinding me. It took a minute or two for my eyes to adjust, then I decided to take a look around the perfect city I was supposedly helping to create. It wasn't like I had anything better to do.

It was morning again … or at least it was a new day. It was hard to tell how fast time went in this game. There were no clocks, just the rising and setting of the sun to help you keep track. And with the amount of time I'd spent underground so far, who knew how many cycles it had actually been.

THE MUSEUM OF NATURAL BLOCKS

CINEMA

I considered taking the map out, but I wasn't in the mood to go sightseeing so decided to just go for a walk instead, heading back down the street where Max had caught the Boulder Person. There was a woman outside the supermarket, carefully reconstructing the shopfront while another woman picked up the blocks that still littered the road.

"What a mess," she muttered.

I carried on, taking a left at the end of the street, turning on to a road next to a small park where some kids were playing football with a block. For obvious reasons it wasn't going very well. Less healthily there was a fast-food place across the road from it called *Square Meals* that seemed to only sell waffles and square sausage.

The Boulder People must have been down here too, I noticed, as the restaurant was missing its doors. So were several shops nearby.

I followed the trail of destruction all the way down the road, turning a corner at the end and entering another street full of houses. They were pretty much the same as the others I had seen so far in Sublimity, not counting Carl's, and a lot of these ones were missing their doorways too.

A man and a woman were standing outside one of the houses, shaking their heads at the damage.

"What is it about doors that they like to destroy so much?" asked the man.

"Never seem to touch anything else, do they?" agreed the woman.

The Boulder Person from the night before did, I thought to myself. It had destroyed the entire storefront, not just the door. But … wait … now that I thought about it, when Max had first spotted it, the

Boulder Person wasn't destroying anything. It just seemed to be trying to get in. The destruction only happened when the miners showed up and the Boulder Person had to pry itself from the doorway.

I stopped suddenly as the thought took hold of my mind. *The doors in this game are block-person sized. Boulder People are almost twice as big. Could it be that all this destruction was just … accidental?*

Did that change anything, though? What were they planning on doing if they did get into the buildings? Was breaking in any better than breaking things?

I noticed the woman and man whispering to each other, staring in my direction, and I realized I probably looked a bit suspicious just standing there staring into space.

I rushed off up the road. I felt like I was on to something, but I wasn't sure what. I had to go find

Max, he was much better at puzzles than I was.

It wasn't hard to know where to look. In the distance the Great Wall was taking shape. It was so big I'd bet you could see it from anywhere in the city. I figured Max was probably to thank for that.

I headed towards the end that was closest to me. With any luck it was where he was working. As I ran through the streets, I remembered that Max and I hadn't exactly parted on good terms. Maybe I owed him an apology.

I mean, I was pretty sure I was mostly in the right, but there was always the chance that I hadn't handled it as well as I could have.

When I arrived at the wall, I was so busy thinking about what I might say to Max in the (unlikely) event that I really did owe him an apology, that I didn't notice the two figures until I walked into them.

"Ow!" said one of them. "Why don't you watch where you're going?"

"Sorry," I said, looking up. "Oh! Stoneheart? Carl?"

"Flo!" said Carl. "How lovely to see you. To what do we owe the pleasure?"

I frowned. "I came to see Max," I said. "Is he around?"

"Oh yes, he's around," said Carl. "But … er … this is a little awkward – he's asked not to be disturbed."

"Not to be disturbed?" I said. "Why? Is he asleep?"

Carl laughed. "No! Quite the opposite, in fact. I've never seen a boy so full of energy. Just look at the progress he's made on the wall."

I followed the wall as it curved for what looked like miles round the edge of the city. It was taller than any of the buildings and wide enough that you could drive cars up and down it.

"Max did all that himself?" I asked.

"We had made a little start before he got involved. But he's done most of it," Carl admitted. "Such a talented builder. He really threw himself into it after you stormed… I mean, after you left."

"I need to see him," I said.

"Shouldn't you be getting back to your own job?" asked Stoneheart. "Digger will be searching for you."

"Stoneheart, why don't you drive Flo back?" suggested Carl.

"No!" I interjected. It was obvious they were trying to keep me from seeing Max. "I'm not going back to the mine until I speak to Max."

"I'm afraid he really doesn't want to be disturbed," said Carl. "I believe he used the words 'in the zone'."

That did sound like something Max would say, but I didn't care.

"I don't care," I said, letting them know. "Tell Max that I'll be waiting for him at the house you found us in. I won't be mining another block until I speak to him."

And so, once again, I stormed off.

LEVEL 6

The sun was starting to go down again with no sign of Max showing up. I'd waited in the house the entire time and now it was dawning on me that I had probably given Carl exactly what he wanted – for Max to be left alone to build the wall. I could tell from the window that progress was going well. It wouldn't be long until it was finished and it was looking like I wouldn't see Max until then.

So when he burst through the door a few minutes later, I was caught off guard.

"Max?" I said. "You came!"

"Carl said you were here," he said. "Why aren't you at the mine?"

I didn't scowl at Max very often, but this was definitely one of those moments where it was required.

"Because I needed to talk to you," I said. "And I'm sick of mining. Why would anyone create a game where you have to mine all day?"

"Well, we've run out of blocks," he said. "I've been building the wall so fast that the miners haven't been able to keep up with demand."

"Well done you," I said sarcastically. "Maybe you'll get a medal. Oh no, medals are normally round, aren't they? What a shame."

Max looked livid. "I'm only building it this fast so we can get home," he said, raising his voice. "I can't do that, though, if we don't have the blocks. Digger says it's going to take them ages to catch up as his best worker has gone on strike."

"Best worker?" I said, unable to contain a smile. "Digger said that about me? He's nice. I like him."

"What did you want to speak to me about anyway?" said Max, folding his arms.

"Right, yeah," I said. "So you remember that Boulder Person you caught?"

"Of course I remember – it wasn't that long ago,"
Max said, rolling his eyes unnecessarily. "What
about her?"

"Her?" I said.

"Yeah," he said. "I heard Carl and some of the
others talking about her. Her name's Girdy."

"What else did you hear about her?" I asked.

Max shrugged. "Not much," he said. "Apparently she's a big deal in the Boulder People community. Royalty or something, I'm not sure. Stoneheart said it took twenty guards to transfer her to the city prison."

"Is that where she is now?" I asked.

"As far as I know," he said. "I mean, I doubt they would just let her go. Why?"

"I think we should go and speak to her," I said.

Max's face had shifted a bit. Now he looked annoyed *and* confused. "Speak to her? What are you talking about?"

I told him about the supermarket, the café and the houses and the missing doors. When I finished, all Max had to say was, "So?"

"What do you mean 'so'?" I asked. "Don't you

think it's weird that they only damage doorways? Maybe because they can't fit through them? And it's not just the Boulder People. Remember that night we first showed up here and the tentacle person knocked on the door?"

"Octoperson," corrected Max.

"The point is it knocked on the door," I said. "Not destroyed it. Which is what we were told these other communities were doing."

"They are," said Max.

"Yes, but maybe only accidentally," I said. "What if they're just trying to get into the buildings to steal stuff?"

Max laughed. "That's not exactly better is it?"

"Maybe not," I said. "But wouldn't it be a good idea to speak to them and try to find out why they're doing it?"

"No, Flo." Max sighed. "It wouldn't be a good idea for a lot of reasons. One is that the Boulder People are dangerous. Another is that even if I did think it was worth talking to Girdy, you'd never be allowed into the prison to see her. What *would* be a good idea is you going back to work, so we can get that wall built and help Carl complete the perfect city. Then maybe we can get out of here and go back to a world where our bodies don't feel like giant cement blocks!"

I grinned at Max, the way I did whenever I suggested something he thought was a bad idea. He always changed his mind in the end.

"Not this time, Flo," he said. "The answer's no."

I shot Max another scowl. "So you want me to go back to the mine?" I asked.

"Yes!" he said, throwing his hands in the air.

"Fine," I said, walking to the door. "I'll go back to the mine."

"Thank you," he said.

"Yeah, and you go back to your precious wall," I said. "Which is absurd, by the way. Since when did putting walls up ever help make things better?"

"In buildings they help quite a lot," said Max. "They keep the roof up."

"Very funny," I said. "You know what I mean. There's no way that wall will get us out of the game. I think you just enjoy this game so much you're trying to drag it out by wasting time building the wall instead of helping me."

Max looked stunned. "You think I'm dragging it out? Now who's being absurd?"

"Or maybe you just like being better at a game than me for once and now the idea that I'm right and you're wrong is too much for you," I fired back.

Max bit his bottom lip. "Didn't you say you were

going back to the mine?" he said in a cold voice.

We stared at each other, unflinching, until I eventually stormed out, slamming the door behind me. I was going to go back to the mine, but not for the reasons Max wanted me to. The prison would be heavily guarded and Max was right, there was no way I would be allowed in to talk to Girdy.

But there were other ways into the prison apart from the door. I'd have to go back to the mine first, though – I was going to need my pickaxe.

LEVEL 7

"Flo! I'm so glad to see you," said Digger when I walked into the mine. "I've just had Stoneheart in here, threatening to fire me if I can't speed up production of blocks for the wall. Please tell me you're here to work?"

"Sure am," I said. I felt bad about lying to Digger, but I didn't see any other option. "I'm not really up for speaking to people right now, though. I just want to take my pickaxe, find an empty corner of the mine and be left to myself for a few hours, OK?"

"Of course," said Digger, handing me the pickaxe.

"Anything for my top worker. Why don't you take the east side? No one's working there and I'll make sure you aren't disturbed."

"That's great, thanks," I said.

"Here, take this too," he said, handing me a hard hat with a torch built into it. "There aren't many lamps down that end."

I put on the hat, gave Digger a nod and headed to the east side of the mine to put my plan into action.

The next challenge was finding the prison. Fortunately I still had the map Digger had given me so I had a rough idea where it was. However, maps are generally designed to be followed above ground, not below it…

On the first try I overshot the prison by several streets, coming up in the middle of an empty outdoor basketball court. I shook my head at the square hoops before ducking back down.

My second attempt was closer, but this time a little short, coming up in a park across the road from the prison. From here I could see how heavily secured the place was. Guards patrolled the outskirts while others were stationed in watchtowers. My next try had to be spot on. No more mistakes.

I came up right in the middle of the guards' break room, accidentally smashing a table. Several guards were sitting around it drinking coffee, which they all spat out at the sight of me.

"Oops," I said, before disappearing back into the tunnel. I quickly flung a block at the hole to fill it but the damage was already done. I could hear the alarms going off. There was no point in crying over spilt coffee, I was just going to have to move faster than I'd planned.

As I tunnelled further beneath the prison I noticed a strange green glowing box attached to the wall. I'd seen a few of these since I'd started tunnelling. They didn't look like normal blocks, more like something someone had put in place deliberately. If Max had been here, I'm sure he would have been able to tell me. I wondered if they were Easter eggs, but I knew now wasn't the time to investigate.

I tunnelled up again, this time into a cell. Unfortunately it was empty, but at least it gave me an idea of where the other cells were. I tunnelled into a few others but they were all empty as well. So far I had seen more guards than actual prisoners, which I suppose makes sense for a prison in a perfect city.

I found Girdy in the tenth cell, sitting on a bed.

I'd forgotten how big and menacing she was. Now, alone in a small prison cell with her, it came back to me.

"Who are you?" her voice boomed as she looked down at me. Her expression suggested she was deciding whether to stomp on me or not.

"My name's Flo," I said. "We don't have much time, the guards will be here soon."

"Hur-hur," laughed Girdy. "I'm not scared of guards. What you want anyway?"

"I've come to talk to you about the night you were captured," I said.

"I wasn't captured," she shouted, furiously slapping a cement-block fist down on her bed. It left a crack. "I was tricked. It wasn't a fair fight. That little boy used building blocks."

"I seem to remember you having blocks too," I said, sticking up for Max. "You were throwing them at everyone!"

Girdy looked confused. "They weren't building

blocks. They were boulders. Boulders are for chucking, not building. You're not very bright, hur-hur."

Given that I'd just broken into a prison to argue with a highly dangerous giant rock monster, she had a point.

Girdy wasn't finished. "Boulder People don't have building blocks. Boulder People don't have anything. No food. Just boulders. Sublimity has everything."

"That's why you were here?" I said. "You were trying to steal from the shops and the houses?"

Girdy brought her fist crashing down again, leaving another crack in the bed. It wasn't going to withstand much more of that. "We're not thieves," she said. "But we have no choice. Once the stupid wall goes up we won't get anything. We'll die. Not just Boulder People, everyone outside. There'll be nothing left for anyone. I tried to help my people, but I failed. I have to get back to them – they need me."

"I heard you were a queen or something?" I asked.

Girdy sniffed at this. "Huh. I'm not a queen, I'm the democratically elected leader of the Boulder People."

"Like a prime minister or a president?" I asked.

"Dunno. Do they get to throw boulders at people if they don't do what I say?" she asked.

I thought about this. "Maybe," I said. "Wait, I hear something."

I pressed my ear against the cell door. There were voices at the end of the corridor, getting closer. I looked back at Girdy. Despite her terrifying appearance, there was something about her that made me trust her. I knew what I had to do.

"Come on," I said. "I'm getting you out of here."

Girdy looked surprised. "You're breaking me out?" she asked.

"Quick, before I change my mind," I said, dropping back down the hole.

Girdy peered into the hole. "I'm not going to fit," she said.

"Oh, right, sorry," I said, swinging my pickaxe up to break a few more blocks. Girdy jumped down then grabbed a handful of blocks, patching up the hole we'd left.

It was only then that I realized I had no idea where we were going. But Girdy was way ahead of me. She held out a massive hand. "Maybe it's best I take the pickaxe," she said. "We have a long way to go, and I doubt you know the way."

"Where are we going?" I asked.

"Boulder Country," she replied.

LEVEL 8

As Girdy had warned, the journey was a long one. Once she had tunnelled about a mile outside the city, she returned my pickaxe before we resurfaced and walked the rest of the way. What quickly became noticeable was that the further out from the city we went, the bleaker the landscape got. Trees were replaced by rocks, grass by dirt and rivers by sand.

"You see?" Girdy kept saying. "There's nothing out here any more."

Nowhere was this more obvious than in Boulder Country. It wasn't so much a country as a barren wasteland, apart from a series of stone tower blocks. The atmosphere was eerie as we walked through a dishevelled granite entranceway. There were no signs of anyone else, Boulder Person or otherwise. I looked up at one of the tower blocks and for a brief moment I thought I saw eyes looking back at me. I blinked and they were gone.

"Where is everyone?" I whispered.

"Dunno," said Girdy. "OI, YOU LOT! WHERE ARE YOU?"

There was no reply. I was about to mention the face I thought I'd seen when I spotted something out of the corner of my eye. I turned round to see an angry Boulder Person charging out of the nearest tower and straight towards me. Just as I was about to be trampled, Girdy stepped in front of me and the other Boulder Person ran right into her. Girdy was the bigger of the two and didn't budge an inch, while the smaller Boulder Person went tumbling backwards into a heap.

"Dash, is that you?" asked Girdy, staring down at the crumpled Boulder Person. "Why you running into me, you silly boy?"

"I didn't mean to get you," said Dash, sitting up and rubbing his head. "I saw that Block Person walking in with you from my window."

"She's with me," said Girdy. "Her name's Flo. She helped me escape. You hurt her and I knock your block off, OK?"

"OK, Girdy," said Dash, getting to his feet.

"Where is everyone?" asked Girdy.

"They're gone," he said.

"I see that," said Girdy. She looked at me and shook her head. "Sorry about Dash, he's fast but not smart. Dash, WHERE have they gone?"

"Council meeting," he said. "All the other communities are there too. Trying to figure out what to do about the Great Wall."

Girdy turned to me. "All right, then we go."

"How far is it?" I asked.

"Pretty far," admitted Girdy. "But don't worry, we'll get there super-quick. We'll take a catapult."

"Oh, OK, cool," I said. "Sorry, we'll take what now?"

Dash hurried off to a tower and pressed a button on the side. Part of the wall slid up, like a garage door. Inside was exactly what I thought Girdy had said. Dash rolled the wooden catapult out, turning it so that it was in a specific position.

"You can't be serious?" I said. "I'm not getting in that."

"It's a four-day walk," said Girdy.

That *was* a long time, but it probably didn't end with me going splat at the end.

"It's fine," said Girdy, scooping me up in her arms and leaping into the basket.

"Girdy, no!" I said, but before I could say anything else, Dash pulled a lever on the side of the catapult.

PFFFFFFTTTTAAAAANNNNNG!

"ARRRRRRRRRRRRRRRRRR…"

The world beneath us shrank to the size of a

Rubik's cube as we soared above it. Then, moments

later, it started to get bigger again as we plummeted

towards the ground. I closed my eyes.

"...RRRRRRRRGHHHHHHHH!"

BOOOOOOOOOOOOOOOOOOOOM!

I opened my eyes. We were in the middle of an open-roofed theatre. Seated around us and staring were all kinds of different creatures. Some, like the Boulder and Octopeople, I had already seen, but others were new to me, like Werewolves, Mummies and some beings that seemed to be made entirely from ice. I looked down at Girdy's feet, which were surrounded by small craters, left there by her landing.

"Hur-hur," laughed Girdy. "You've really never travelled by catapult?"

"No," I said, shaking a little as she put me down. "I did once do something similar, but it involved a tank. And it was in space. Somehow that felt safer…"

Several Boulder People rushed down from the stands to greet Girdy.

"We thought we never see you again," said one of them.

"Maybe you wouldn't have, if Flo here hadn't broken me out," she said, giving me a friendly, but still quite hard, slap on the back.

"Girdy, good to have you here," said someone else, this time not a Boulder Person. It was an Octoperson just like the one Max and I had seen when we first jumped in. In fact—

"Hey, I know you," she said, looking right at me. "I saw you in that house in Sublimity. I do hope I didn't frighten you, I was just searching for some food and I saw your light on. My name is Ollie."

"Ollie the Octoperson?" I said.

Ollie sighed. "Yes, it's a big problem in the Octoperson community that every one of us is called Ollie. It gets very confusing, especially at family dinners."

"I'll bet," I said, glancing nervously at the scary-looking monsters in the crowd. "What are you doing here?"

"This is an emergency meeting of the Community Council," she said in a serious tone. "Our communities are at breaking point. There aren't enough resources for us all to survive, while the city of Sublimity has far more than it could ever need."

I opened my mouth to argue this, remembering how Carl had told us that resources were scarce when Max and I built our house. But no words came out as it dawned on me that if this was true, how come Carl was living in a massive mansion? And I'd been in the mines, so I knew there were plenty of resources down there. Not to mention how much more there would be if people stopped building that stupid wall.

"We're forced to steal from them," Ollie continued. "But when the wall is complete, that will no longer be an option."

"What about tunnelling in?" suggested Girdy. "We already made some pretty good tunnels. Or we could use catapults?"

"We shouldn't have to," shouted someone from the crowd. I looked round but couldn't tell who had spoken.

"That's Lord Obscuro," said Ollie, pointing towards a person in the crowd. He was wearing a black suit but he had no face, and I couldn't help but flinch at the sight of him. "The leader of the Faceless People. He has a point, though. Even if we can get past the wall, we can't keep going on like this, living off scraps."

A person with what looked like a cabbage for a head stood up. "The State of Vegetania proposes war against Sublimity."

My jaw dropped. "War? Wait, slow down. Shouldn't we try talking to Sublimity first?"

The theatre fell silent and all eyes, and non-eyes in the case of the Faceless People, were on me.

"Talk?" said the Cabbage Person. "The people there see us as monsters. They won't talk to us. They chase us with pitchforks and fire."

She had a point. They were an intimidating-looking bunch. Just the thought of speaking in front of them had made my mouth go dry, let alone seeing them breaking into the city in the dead of night. But I knew I had to speak. "I know their leader, Carl," I said. "I could talk to him. This is clearly a big misunderstanding. Carl can be a bit … difficult, but he just wants his city to be safe. When I tell him what's happening, he'll realize the way to do that is to let you in, not keep you out. It's got to be worth a try?"

"The Faceless People stand with the State of Vegetania," said Lord Obscuro. "We second the motion for war."

"Then let's vote on it," said one of the Ice People, who was shivering uncontrollably. "But quickly – I'm freezing."

"I told you to bring a jacket," said the Ice Person next to him. "But nooo…"

I looked at Ollie and Girdy. "Please, my best friend is still in the city."

"Those in favour of war, raise your hand," continued the Cabbage Person. Almost all the hands in the theatre shot up, apart from Ollie's and Girdy's.

"Motion carried," said the Cabbage Person. "Send word to the communities to start disassembling all buildings and structures at once. We need those blocks for war. Now we must discuss battle strategies. The girl said she has made tunnels underneath the city. We could use those."

Ollie put a tentacle on my shoulder. "Follow me," she said, leading Girdy and me out through a side door. "You really think you can get Sublimity to talk?"

"Maybe," I said. "I'm not their favourite person right now. I didn't exactly break Girdy out of jail undetected. But I could try."

"Hmm. I guess it's the best chance we have of avoiding war," said Ollie. "Worryingly however, the communities agreed pretty quickly to fight, and it normally takes them ages to agree on anything, so you might not have much time… We can get you close to the city, but you'll have to find your own way in."

I held up my pickaxe. "I can do that," I said. "How are you going to get me close, though? And please don't say by catapult."

"Er… How about a trebuchet?" asked Ollie.

"What's a treh-boo-shay?" I asked suspiciously.

"A fancy word for catapult," said Girdy.

I sighed. "I thought it might be."

LEVEL 9

Since I didn't have the ability to land safely like the
Boulder People, Girdy had taken a few minutes to
set the catapult – or trebuchet – so that I'd land in a
lake near the city. What she failed to tell me was it
was a mud lake.

Video Game Tip: Video-game mud is still gross.

After pulling myself out of the lake and shaking off as much mud as I could, I made my way towards the city, my feet squelching. After a few minutes I saw it and gasped. The wall looked complete. Digger's team must have stepped up their mining efforts.

Max had done a great job, as far as building a wall went. I had been proven right, though – we hadn't left the game. Unsurprisingly, this didn't make me feel any better.

I raised my pickaxe and smashed it to the ground. If I had got better at anything since we arrived, it was definitely building underground tunnels in a hurry.

What I hadn't yet got the hang of was figuring out how to come out of those tunnels without ending up surrounded by City Guards. Of all the places I wanted to tunnel into, the annual Sublimity City Guards' cheese and wine party was pretty low on the list. Yet here I was. I probably should have checked the map.

A dozen hands grabbed me and yanked me out of the hole.

"There she is," said a voice I recognized. "The jail-breaker."

"Stoneheart!" I said, realizing there might be a silver lining to ending up here. "Am I glad to see you."

"I bet you are," he said. "I. Bet. You. Are."

"You need to take me to see Carl," I said. "Right away. This can't wait!"

Stoneheart looked around the room at his fellow guards and chuckled. "Can you believe this one? Refuses to contribute to society, steals an official Sublimity council pickaxe, breaks a hardened criminal out of jail, tunnels into a guard-only event and then proceeds to give orders to me – Captain of the City Guards. There's only one place I'm taking you, young lady, and that's straight to jail."

"You don't understand!" I said. But it was hopeless. Moments later I was bundled into the back of a police van and driven back to the same prison I had broken Girdy out of. I wasn't sure what was worse – Stoneheart refusing to listen to me or having to ride in another square-wheeled vehicle.

Actually it was pretty clear – the second one was worse.

Fortunately I didn't have to go to Carl. He came to me, along with Max, shortly after I was put in prison.

"Flo!" shouted Max, rushing over to the bars.

"Max!" I replied. "I'm so glad to see you."

"Me too," said Max. "They say you broke that Boulder Person out of jail. I told them they must have it wrong."

"No," I said. "They're right, Max, I did. But I had a good reason."

"Well, I'm all ears," said Carl.

"OK, so it started when I noticed that the monsters only seemed to damage doorways…"

"There's nothing out there any more," I said, five minutes later. "Just a bunch of desperate communities living on the edge. Sublimity could help them."

"Help them?" said Carl. "But they've continually tried to destroy our city."

"They're not trying to destroy Sublimity," I said. "They're just trying to stay alive. Some of them happen to be a bit clumsy. Now they're talking about starting a war."

Carl looked horrified. "A war? With us?"

"I don't think they really want to," I said, trying not to alarm him. "But with the wall going up they believe they're out of options. The Boulder and Octopeople let me come back to see if I could convince Sublimity to help them. Sublimity has so much, I think if you could offer them aid or maybe even let them live here they'd be so grateful."

Carl turned to Max. "You've been quiet so far, Max," he said. "What do you think?"

"I think…" said Max, "that I owe you an apology, Flo. I thought building the wall would create the perfect city, but after what you've told us, how could a city be perfect if people are dying outside it? We need to help them."

Carl stroked his goatee, appearing to think it over.

"Of course, you're both right," he said. "We must help the outsiders."

"Brilliant!" I said. "I knew you couldn't be as uptight as you seemed."

"You … think I'm uptight?" asked Carl, looking hurt.

"Um, no," I said, trying to backtrack. "Sorry, Carl, I didn't mean—"

"Ha, I'm messing with you, Flo." Carl laughed. "I know I can come across as uptight sometimes. Most of the time, in fact. It's just I really do care about this city, you know? I've spent my entire life trying to make it the best it can be."

"I understand," I said.

"Good," he said. "But this war – are the communities on their way now?"

"I think so," I said. "They said something about

having to break down their buildings first to get blocks to fight with but once that's done they'll be on their way."

"How are they planning on getting into the city?" he asked.

"Through the tunnels," I said. "The ones Girdy and I dug to escape."

Carl nodded as he reached into his pocket and took out a set of keys. "Then there's no time to lose. Let's get you out of there."

Carl pushed a key into the lock and turned it, before sliding the door open.

I hadn't even taken a step when Max let out a yell as Carl shoved him from behind, pushing him into the cell. He collided with me and we tumbled to the floor. Carl meanwhile slammed the cell door shut, locking us both in.

"Carl, what are you doing?" shouted Max.

"What I always do," he said, grinning maliciously. "Making the city the best it can be by getting rid of its enemies. Starting with you two and ending with those fools outside the wall."

I scrambled to my feet. "You weasel," I yelled.

"We're not your enemies! I mean, we weren't. We will be if you don't let us out."

"Yes, I'm terribly frightened," yawned Carl. "But in a way I am sorry it's come to this. Sublimity does owe you both an awful lot, after all. Max, it almost goes without saying, for building the Great Wall that will keep those horrible monsters out of my nice clean city. But you too, Flo. Perhaps we owe you our greatest thanks."

"Me? What for?" I asked.

"Why, for tipping us off about the communities' plans for war." He laughed, as he started walking away. "Because now, when they come, we'll be ready for them."

LEVEL 10

Despite the hopelessness of our situation, Max started laughing.

"What's so funny?" I asked.

"Oh, nothing," he said. "I was just thinking that every time I go along with your ideas I end up in trouble. But the first time I don't listen to you, I wind up in jail. I can't win!"

"That's exactly why you should always listen to me," I said. "At least then when things go wrong you have someone else to blame."

Max nodded. "I hadn't thought about it like that!"

We grinned at each other.

"I'm sorry, Flo," said Max. "You were right, I was enjoying the game too much. I guess I liked being the expert for once. I thought I'd be the one who would get us out of the game this time."

"This time?" I said. "We got out of the last game together. And we'll get out of this one together too. Because we're a team, you and I. A partnership. Co-op mode for life."

Max punched the air triumphantly. "Yeah!"

"All right then, we're agreed," I said. "Now you just need to come up with a plan to get us out of here."

"Me?" said Max. "What about us being a team?"

"You said you were the expert!" I retorted. "So how do we get out of a prison cell in *Blocktopia*?"

"I don't know," said Max. "You're the one who's already done it."

"That was when I had a pickaxe," I said. "Funnily enough they didn't let me keep it when they threw me in here. Can't you just build us something to get us out? A bulldozer or something?"

Max looked around. "We wouldn't have space," he said. "Even if we did I don't have any blocks left. I used every last one building the wall. And without a pickaxe to mine, we won't be able to get any more."

"We're stuck here?" I asked.

The defeated look on Max's face said it all. "Pretty much," he said. "Unless by some miracle you happen to have something else that can get us out of here."

My eyes lit up. How could I have forgotten? I put my hand in my pocket and pulled out a small block.

"Something like this?" I asked, as a pale red glow lit up the dark cell.

"A firebrick!" cried Max. "From when we built the house? Flo, you're a genius!"

"Well, obviously that's true," I said. "But I think in this case the real geniuses are the guards who lock people up without checking if they happen to be carrying explosive firebricks with them."

"I'm going to try not to think about the fact that you've been carrying an explosive around in your pocket for days," said Max.

"That's probably for the best," I said before lobbing the firebrick at the wall.

Video Game Tip: As well as being explosive, firebricks have one other interesting property – they're surprisingly bouncy.

"Flo, look out!" yelled Max, diving at me as the red block smacked off the wall and rebounded back towards me. We tumbled out of the way just in time to see the firebrick bounce off the floor and into the cell door, which it exploded, taking the entire entrance with it.

"Whoops," I said, as we got to our feet.

"Come on, let's get out of here!" yelled Max.

"Watch out for guards," I said, hurrying out.

I thought the explosion might have caught their attention, but as we made our way through the prison it became clear there was no one about.

"Carl must have them all preparing for the ambush," I said when we reached the prison exit.

As Max went to push open the door, I put a blocky hand on his shoulder. "Hold on, wait here," I said, and rushed back into the prison. A few moments later I reappeared, armed with my pickaxe. "I saw them put it in a property room when they brought me in. I also found this." I handed him the tiny chest.

"Blocks," he said. "Nice one."

We left the prison, stepping cautiously out into the night before sneaking stealthily through the shadowy streets. But once again, it quickly became obvious there was no one around. Just as I began to worry that our problem was not going to be avoiding people but finding them, we heard the cries.

We followed the sounds of people screaming and shouting for several blocks until we turned the corner into a street just off City Square. I grabbed Max and pulled him behind a parked car before anyone spotted us.

The first thing we saw was the hundreds of guards assembled in the square carrying pitchforks. They appeared to be surrounding something. There among them I spotted a nervous Digger. Brick was a few guards along from him.

"It looks like they've made everyone in the city a guard," said Max.

There were large TV screens attached to the sides of some of the buildings in the square and on them we could see what the guards were surrounding: frightened monsters of all kinds – Octo, Boulder, Ice and Faceless People, Vegetanians, Werewolves and Mummies.

Carl was there, perched on a raised platform. But just in case anyone couldn't make him out, he and his grinning goatee were being projected on to one of the massive screens.

"But I didn't build a tunnel here!" I said.

"They must have rerouted it," suggested Max. "I suppose it makes sense to have everyone come out in a big open space like City Square, where the guards could easily surround them. The guards probably hid and waited until everyone was up before making their move."

"What do we do?" I said. I knew if it were left to me, we'd go running straight into a fight. But we had to be smarter. Max was better at puzzles and strategy and this was a situation that required some thought and planning.

"I think we have to go and fight them," said Max.

"What?" I said. "That's the sort of stupid idea I'd come up with!"

"We won't be doing it alone," he said. "We'll have help."

"The communities?" I said. "They're not exactly in a position to lend a hand."

"They will be in a few minutes, though," he said. "All they need is a distraction."

"And you're going to make one?" I asked.

Max grinned as he took out the chest of blocks. "You better believe I'm going to make one."

LEVEL 11

"Fools!" Carl shouted at his prisoners. "Did you really think you'd be able to attack my city? Attack me, the Architect? Sublimity is the greatest city ever created. It could never fall to the likes of you. But since you all want to live in it so badly, at least you can take comfort in the fact that you will spend the rest of your miserable little lives here. Unfortunately, it'll be behind bars. Because after tonight none of you will ever set another foot or tentacle in my perfect cit— Wait, what's that?"

The guards and monsters fell silent as everyone

followed Carl's gaze towards the opposite end of the square. No one seemed to be sure what they were supposed to be looking at, though, as all anyone could see was a pleasant fountain.

"The ... fountain?" asked Stoneheart.

"Exactly!" yelled Carl.

"Well ... it's a ... fountain," said Stoneheart, displaying the same confusion as the rest of the guards.

"I know it's a fountain, you fool," snapped Carl, climbing down off the platform and marching towards the fountain, as Stoneheart and some of the guards followed behind him. "But look at it! It's nothing like the Tutorials. It's the wrong colour for a start. It should be seashell. This is eggshell. And every fountain should have a maximum of one statue, which should be a representation of me.

This one has two statues that don't look anything like me. If anything they look like…"

Carl squinted at the fountain for a moment, before his eyes suddenly bulged. He spun round and yelled: "The kids! They've escaped! They're here!"

Confusion spread through the guards as their heads turned every way, looking for us. But of course that meant they weren't watching their prisoners. And it was all the prisoners needed.

The Boulder People smashed a path through the guards, letting the other monsters break free. Then they started building.

The Octopeople quickly assembled a large wooden machine that looked a bit like

a spinning top except it had eight arms with concrete blocks at the end of them. Someone flicked a switch on it, gave it a little shove then dived out of the way as it started spinning, getting faster and faster while moving across the square, its flailing arms whacking guards as it passed.

A little worryingly, given their lack of eyes, the Faceless People had constructed cannons, which they were using to fire Boulder People into the guards. To be fair to them, though, they were hitting their targets.

Meanwhile Carl was struggling to keep his composure. "Stop them!" he yelled. "They're ruining everything!"

It seemed like a good time for Max and me to show ourselves. We burst out of the fountain.

Carl spun back round. "You!"

"Us," I agreed.

"It's a Trojan fountain," said Max.

"Look what you two have done!" said Carl, pointing towards the battle.

"You can stop this right now," I said. "You can make peace."

Carl snorted as he laughed. "Peace? With them? Never. You think their stupid contraptions are enough to stop me? I'm the Architect. I wrote the Tutorials. Everything we need is in there."

Carl sprinted off towards Stoneheart and a group

of guards who had just managed to take down one of the Octopeople's whirling bashers with their pitchforks. I could see the red cover of the Tutorials in Carl's hands as he pointed to a page. Stoneheart and the others nodded and they quickly started throwing blocks together, building what looked like a long battering ram. Each of the guards grabbed one of the handles that ran along its sides and started running towards the monsters, bashing loads of them out of the way.

Carl had plenty of other tricks up his sleeve, directing guards to build all manner of things like giant siege towers for them to hide behind, as they pushed back the monsters and huge crossbows that fired flaming arrows.

"I remember when this used to be a relaxing game." Max sighed.

"Come on, we have to help," I said.

Max nodded. "I'm going to need more blocks," he said.

"I'm on it," I said, holding up my pickaxe.

We got to work – me mining blocks by smashing as much as I could. Which was a lot.

And Max, he was in his element.

Finally free from having to build things from Carl's book, Max let his creative juices flow. So naturally he built himself a giant rhinoceros-shaped vehicle, which he immediately used to plough straight through the guards' siege towers.

As I watched him go, I felt the ground tremble a little behind me. I spun round with my pickaxe but was relieved when I saw Girdy smiling down at me.

"Flo, good to see you," she said.

"You too, Girdy," I said. "Sorry I couldn't stop all this."

"It's not your fault," she said, as she flung a boulder at a nearby group of guards, knocking them over like pins in a bowling alley. "Don't suppose you have spare blocks, though?"

I nodded and handed her enough to keep her and some of her troops busy for a while.

I realized that the other communities needed more supplies too so that became my job, disappearing underground and popping up where needed. Over the next few hours I provided blocks that allowed:

- the Mummies to build a makeshift medical facility

- the Werewolves to build a fleet of cube-wheeled motorbikes

- the Ice People to build snow cannons

- the Cabbage-head Vegetanians to construct a massive motorized fire-breathing pumpkin

Max finally reappeared as dawn was breaking, now in a large block-based exoskeleton suit with gigantic robotic claws. He seemed to have come to the same conclusions as me.

"This is pointless," he said. "No one's winning. If this keeps going we could be here for years. There's got to be a better way to resolve this."

"You're right," I said, glancing up at the TV screens.

They'd been damaged in the battle. "I might have an idea, but I need to get everyone's attention. Can you fix those screens?"

Max seemed unsure. "Possibly," he said. "But it might take a while with all the groups fighting near them. And even once I've fixed one it'll be a challenge to stop anyone breaking it before I've had a chance to fix another one."

My heart sank, but Max hadn't finished speaking. "If you just need everyone to hear you," he said, climbing out of his robot suit, "then I do have one idea…"

LEVEL 12

"STOP FIGHTING!!!"

Max's enormous block megaphone worked an absolute treat. Guards and monsters alike froze on the spot as my words thundered across the square. But I knew that I wouldn't have their attention for long. I had to get this right.

"You know, I never used to understand this game… Er, I mean world," I said, quickly correcting myself. "Give me a spaceship and I could take on the entire universe by myself. Stick me in a go-kart and I'll win the grand prix. Dump me in a maze and ask me to eat pellets while some ghosts chase me and … well, that's weird, but I'll get the job done. Give me a few blocks and tell me to build something? I don't know where to start."

I could tell from a few anxious faces in the crowd that I should probably get to the point, so I carried on.

"But just look around you," I said. "Look at the incredible things you've built. I think I get it now. It's about using your imagination and working with other people to create something amazing. But just think for a minute how brilliant it would be if instead of building things to destroy each other, you worked together to build something to make all of your lives better."

There was a murmur throughout the crowd, but it was none other than Stoneheart who made his voice heard. "Like what?" he yelled.

"Like a city for everyone," I said.

There was a long pause, then he said, "With that lot?"

"Why not?" I asked.

"I mean … I have to admit that giant pumpkin with the flames was pretty cool," said Stoneheart.

"Thank you!" shouted a Vegetanian.

"But it's hardly the sort of thing we need here, is it?" asked Stoneheart.

The Vegetanians grumbled before one of them spoke. "We can build other things, you know," she said. "Come on, let's show him."

Within seconds the Vegatanians had put together a one-bedroom tomato-shaped bungalow.

Stoneheart looked impressed. "Not bad," he said.

"We can do better than that," shouted the Werewolves, quickly knocking up a medium-sized dog grooming centre.

The Boulder People threw together a wrecking-ball crane, the Faceless People an optician's and the Octopeople a Ferris wheel.

"Well, I'm sold," said Stoneheart, as he joined the queue that had somehow already formed for the Ferris wheel.

"NO, NO, NO!" screamed a voice in the crowd. Of course, it could only be one person. Carl shoved his way through till he was standing right in front of me and Max. He looked furious.

"Guards, tear down those hideous things at once," he demanded. He held up the Tutorials. "This is my city. I am the Architect. If it's not written in here then it doesn't belong."

A tentacle snapped through the air, snatching the red book out of Carl's hands.

"Hey, give that back," shouted Carl.

"Let's have a look at these Tutorials anyway," said Ollie, flicking through them. About halfway through she stopped and frowned. "Wait a minute. Where did you get this from?"

Carl suddenly looked sheepish. "Er... Sorry?"

Ollie held up the book. "Designs for a windmill and wind turbines," she said. "These are Octopeople inventions."

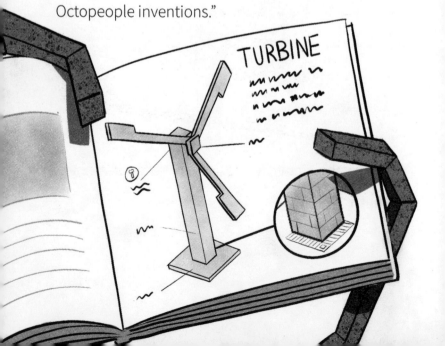

"Anyone could have come up with those,"
said Carl.

Ollie continued flicking through the book until
it was snatched from her hands by Girdy. "Hey!"
she said. "These are instructions on how to build
concrete car parks. These are ancient Boulder
People plans."

Carl threw his hands in the air. "Do you people even
have cars?"

Girdy paused. "No," she said. "But that's beside the point. You stole this."

"Steal? Ha!" said Carl, looking a little flustered. "From you? How absurd."

"Not just us," said Girdy, scanning the book. "From everyone. I recognize all kinds of buildings from other groups."

"Carl, is that true?" asked Stoneheart, reluctantly leaving the Ferris wheel queue.

Carl looked like he was going to deny it, before letting out a sigh. "OK, fine, so maybe I did borrow a few ideas from my years travelling the world. Everywhere I went I saw the same things – small towns and villages with nothing going for them but an idea or two. The more places I saw, the more I realized that if you took those ideas and brought them together, you could create the ultimate city.

And I knew that only I could make this vision a reality. So I began writing down the ideas, learning how to build them, creating the Tutorials. There was just one problem."

"You had to find the right location," said Max.

"Exactly," agreed Carl. "One of the other things I noticed on my travels was how scarce materials were. It's why none of the communities ever grew that big. There simply wasn't enough for everyone. That changed when I found this site. It had everything. Plentiful trees, rocky hills, mines full of silver, iron and gold. It was amazing no one had found it before. I returned to the village I was born in and convinced a small group to come with me to build Sublimity."

From the way Stoneheart nodded at this, I guessed he was part of that group. "You never told us any of this," he said. "You just told us you'd found a great place to build a city. You kept coming up with these amazing building ideas, we thought you were a genius. And you warned us about all the horrible monsters you came across and how we should be terrified of them."

"Uh, hello?" Carl said, pointing at Girdy and Ollie. "And I *am* a genius. Thanks to me you live in the greatest city the world has ever known. I knew that given half a chance those monsters would try to take everything I built."

"So everything in the Tutorials came from the other communities?" said Stoneheart. "It sounds to me like they're owed. I say we let them in!"

There was a short pause as the communities and Block People thought this over, followed by a deafening roar of approval.

"No!" screamed Carl. "This is my city! Mine! I'm in charge!"

It was pretty clear that was no longer the case. Block People and monsters were already hugging and shaking hands or claws or tentacles. Everyone was full of smiles except for the Faceless People, who had a good excuse, and Carl.

Surely even he would have to admit that he was finished as a leader.

But he didn't admit it. What he did was to reach into his pocket and take out a small handheld cube with a square red button on it. Max and I were the only ones who saw him – the others were too busy celebrating.

"What's that?" I asked.

"I am the Architect," he said, in a cold voice. "I always have a plan. Even for this."

"Your time's up, Carl," said Max. "Don't do anything stupid."

"If my time's up," he said, "then everyone's time is up."

As Carl pushed the button, my mind flashed back to the night I broke Girdy out of prison. The strange green glowing boxes I kept finding underground.

Not lights.

Not Easter eggs.

Explosives.

Seconds later the ground started to shake.

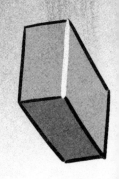

LEVEL 13

"You're blowing up your own city?" I yelled at Carl, as the ground beneath us continued to rumble. He had this creepy grin on his face. "That's right, *my* city," he said. "I'd rather see it destroyed than let anyone else have it."

"But *you're* still in the city," said Max.

Carl's mouth opened and closed a few times. In the distance buildings started to fall down and cracks began to appear

at our feet. Then Carl seemed to realize what he'd done. His eyes almost popped out, the colour drained from his face and I could swear his goatee turned grey in an instant. "What have I done?" he screamed. "Please, you have to get me out of here."

Girdy lunged towards him, shaking her massive fists.

"No, Girdy," I said, putting myself between her and Carl. "We don't have time. We have to get everyone to safety."

She frowned but nodded. "We can build catapults?" she said.

"There's too many people, it'll take forever," said Ollie. "We should build cars."

"Look around you," said Stoneheart. "The ground is breaking up too fast, we'd never get out in time."

The different groups continued to argue among themselves about the best way to escape. Meanwhile the city was crumbling. Time was running out. I looked at Max, but he was staring at the ground.

No, not the ground – he was staring at the

Tutorials. Discarded, they lay open at the page Ollie had pointed out earlier, describing how to build a windmill.

"Of course!" said Max, as if he had spotted the most obvious thing in the world. He sprang into action, throwing blocks around like he was speed-running *Tetris*. In less than a minute it was complete.

"What's that?" asked Girdy.

"It's a helicopter," I said. "It's like a windmill that can fly."

"Fly?" said Ollie. "You mean … in the air?"

"Exactly," said Max. "We'll need more, though."

"You'll have them," said Stoneheart.

"We'll help too," said Girdy.

Digger pushed his way through the crowd. "They'll need blocks," he said, looking at me. "We'll have to be careful, mind, with the place collapsing and all."

We set to work: me, Digger and the crew of former miners turned guards turned miners again supplying the bricks and Max, the monsters and the rest of the Block People constructing the helicopters. The only person not doing anything useful was Carl, who was blubbing like a baby.

Within minutes, hundreds of helicopters had been built. Each time one was finished, it was quickly filled, half with Block People and half with monsters, before flying to safety outside the city. Carl tried to sneak himself on each time. And each time Girdy would grab him and fling him back to the ground.

By the time the last helicopter was built it was just me, Max, Girdy and Carl left.

"All right, get in," I said to Carl, who didn't need

any encouragement. We climbed in after him and I took the pilot's seat – I mean, if I could fly a spaceship through a galactic battle, then a helicopter shouldn't be much trouble. I took off just in time to watch the square collapse into the ground, along with the rest of the city.

"My beautiful city," wept Carl.

"You are the thickest person I've ever met," said Girdy, shaking her head. "And I'm made of rocks."

I followed the other helicopters, eventually landing on a patch of land beyond where the city used to be. Girdy jumped out first then helped Max down.

Max squirmed a little. "I … er … meant to say sorry about the whole putting you into prison thing."

Girdy glared at him for a few seconds before breaking out into a grin. "Hur-hur, you're OK," she said. "Not like that one… Hey!"

I saw Girdy point towards me as Carl suddenly barged into the cockpit and flung me into the passenger seat.

"Now what are you doing?" I shouted.

"Escaping, obviously," he said, pulling on the lever.

There was a roar from the helicopter, but oddly it didn't move at all.

"What's going on?" asked a panicked Carl.

We both looked over our shoulders through the doorway. Outside, Girdy had a hand firmly clamped around one of the helicopter's landing skids.

"Hey, hold it there would you, Girdy?" I asked, hopping out of the passenger door. "I want to have a go at building something for once."

"This I have to see," said Max.

I took out my pickaxe and began breaking up the helicopter, re-forming its parts until I got it just right.

I stood back and admired my creation.

"A catapult?" asked Max. "Nice!"

Carl, who had gone from sitting in a pilot's seat to

sitting in a catapult's bucket, was not as impressed.

"You can't be serious?" he said.

"Girdy, would you like to do the honours?"
I asked.

"With pleasure," she said, whacking the catapult's
lever.

We watched Carl fly through the air for miles, until
he was just a speck, then gone.

"I'm actually starting to like this game," I said.

The three of us walked over to the others and looked out over the remains of Sublimity.

"Now what we do?" asked Girdy.

Max and I looked at each other with confused expressions. "Isn't it obvious?" asked Max.

"You rebuild!" I said.

"But this time you build a city for everyone," Max added.

"It'll take forever," said Girdy.

"You guys just evacuated an entire city in minutes," I pointed out. "Working together, you'll have it built in no time."

"They're right," said Ollie, punching several of her tentacles in the air.

"Well, what are we waiting for?" asked Stoneheart.

Max and I hung back as the monsters and Block

People set off towards their new future.

When they were out of earshot I turned to Max. "I know what I just said, but seriously – it's going to take them ages. We're going to be stuck here for years waiting for the perfect city."

"I thought you were starting to like this game?" Max laughed.

This was another of those occasions when I felt the need to scowl at him.

"Anyway, I don't think it will be as long as that," said Max. "He probably didn't mean it, but I think Carl got something right."

"Really?" I asked, unable to imagine what that might be.

"Don't you remember what he told us?" asked Max. "The secret to the perfect city?"

I smiled. "The people."

"Exactly," said Max. "Whatever the new city ends up looking like, it's got the people it needs. It's already perfect."

In the distance, everyone had gathered around Girdy to watch as she placed a single cement block amongst the rubble: the first brick laid in a brand-new city. And then the world turned black and Max and I were once again staring at two giant neon words:

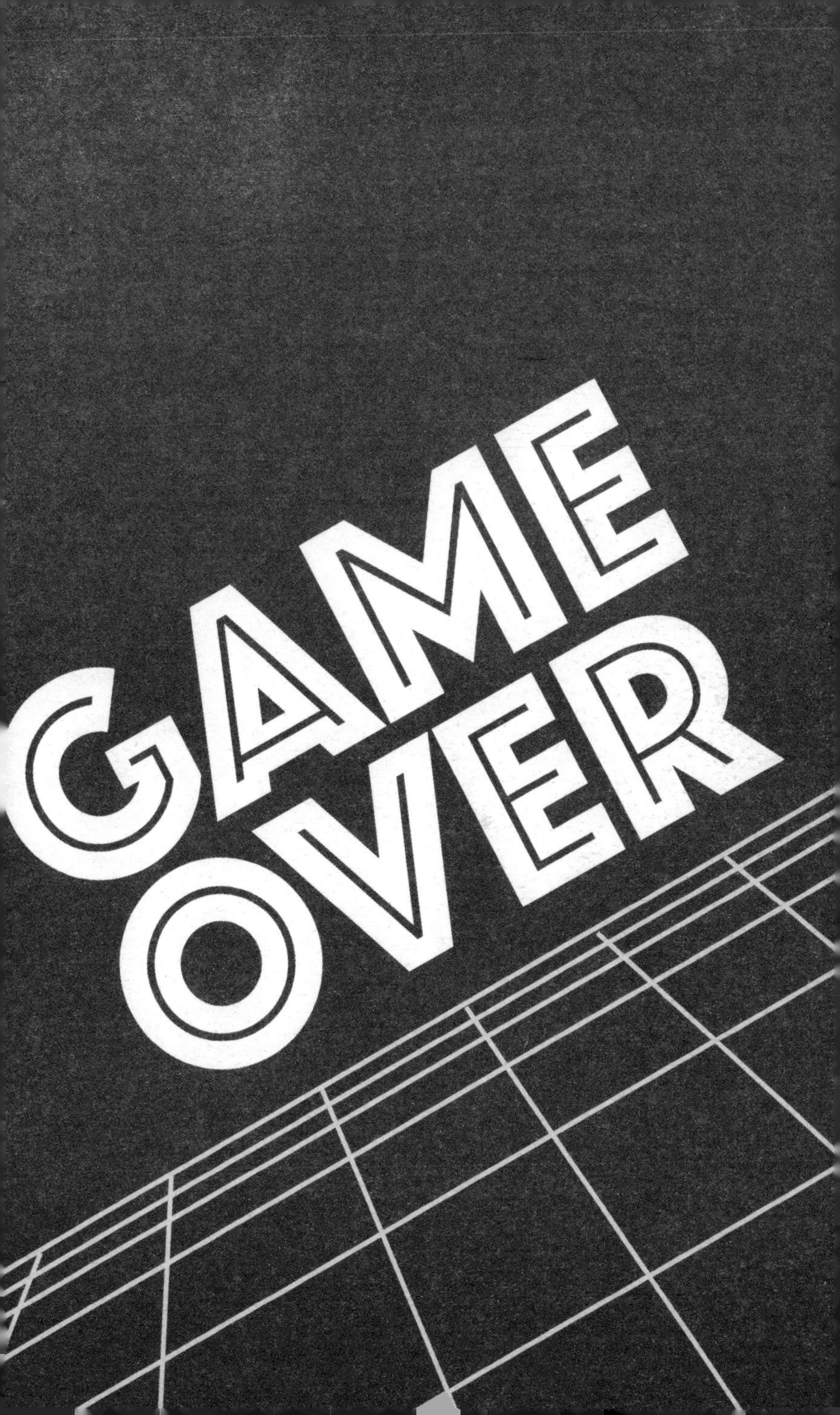
GAME
OVER

BONUS LEVEL

We respawned in a forest. The trees were bright and colourful and the grass no longer looked hard and flat. Most importantly, though, nothing was made of blocks.

"Where are we now?" asked Max.

"I'm not sure," I said. "It feels more like a cartoon than a video game."

"Ha, your hair is all pointy," said Max.

"So is yours," I said. "At least we're not made of blocks any more. I was starting to forget what a circle looked like."

With no clue what to do, we started walking through the forest, eventually coming to a small stream.

"Hey, look," I said, pointing at a little creature sipping water at the edge. It was about the size of a rabbit, but yellow like a baby chick and about four times as fluffy. It must have heard us approaching as it turned round to look at us, displaying the cutest, widest eyes I'd ever seen. Instead of being alarmed, it gave us a big friendly smile.

"It's like someone invented the most adorable thing they could imagine," said Max.

The creature hopped over to us. Somehow, its smile got even bigger, and even cuter.

"Awww!" we said as we reached down and petted it.

It was then that the creature opened its mouth to

about ten times the size of its body and swallowed
us whole.

To be continued...

LEVEL UP!

UP!

BEAST BATTLES

**COMING SOON TO
A BOOKSHOP NEAR YOU!**

TURN THE PAGE FOR A SNEAK PEEK AT FLO AND MAX'S NEXT ADVENTURE...

LEVEL 1

"Max? You still alive?" I asked.

"I think so," he replied, sitting up and wiping drool off his glasses. "You?"

"Of course I am, I just asked you," I said.

"Oh yeah, right," he said. "Sorry, I wasn't thinking straight. Probably from being eaten."

It was a bit much to take in. Especially when the thing that had eaten you was the size of a large bunny. On the other hand, Max and I had seen and experienced quite a lot of strange things recently. Ever since a machine my mum had built accidentally transported us into a video game, we'd flown in epic space battles, been catapulted across a world made of blocks, and helped improve countless virtual lives along the way. When you think about it, is being eaten by a harmless-looking fluffy animal really that odd?

Actually, yes. Yes, it is.

"It's surprisingly big in here, don't you think?" asked Max.

"You're right," I agreed, staring around the cavern that was the inside of the creature that had eaten us. The walls were soft and fleshy, and it was a bit like being inside a hollowed-out giant pink flan. "I guess we're in another game, then. One involving creatures with huge appetites."

"No kidding," said Max, pointing at some of the other things the creature had snacked on.

They included:

- a grandfather clock
- a STOP sign
- a variety of trees and assorted shrubbery
- a couch
- tyres of several different sizes
- a small boat
- an entire fish tank, complete with fish

"What's that thing there?" asked Max, pointing at a small round hole in the middle of all the junk. It was black and swirling and kind of gooey, like a really thick soup.

"I don't know," I admitted. "Could be a wall glitch.

Best not go near it."

Max nodded slowly. "How are we going to get out of here, then?"

"You're not going anywhere, so pipe down already," a voice boomed.

Max and I looked around. "Who said that?" I asked.

"Who do you think?" replied the voice. It sounded female. "Me. The thing that ate you."

"You can hear us?" asked Max.

"Of course I can hear you," she said. "I'm

right here."

"As you can hear us," I said, "you'd better just go ahead and spit us out. Right now!"

The creature made a snorting sound that caused her insides to jiggle, almost knocking us over. "Or what?" She laughed.

"Or… Or…" I said, trying to think of something. "OK, I don't know what. But you should let us go."

"I'm afraid I disagree," she said.

"Disagree?" I repeated, stroking my chin, an idea starting to form. "That's it. Max, I've got it."

"You have?" he asked.

"We're basically her food, right?" I said. "And we're in disagreement. Now, what normally happens when food disagrees with someone?"

Max considered this for a moment. "They throw up. But Flo, that expression doesn't literally mean the person is arguing with their lunch."

I rolled my eyes. "Obviously I know that. But the principle is the same. We're going to make her throw up."

"You wouldn't…" said the creature, though she didn't sound convinced.

"We'll have to disagree on that too," I said, as I started jumping around in her stomach. "Come on, Max."

Max joined me, flinging himself into the soft mushy walls as I repeatedly stomped on the floor. After half a minute or so of this there was a loud groaning noise.

"Ooooooh, please … stop!" said the creature. "I think I'm going to…"

There was a loud retch.

Then another.

And another.

And then:

"BLEEUUUURRRRGGHH!!!"

We shot out into the bright daylight and landed in a crumpled heap on the grass, covered in drool. I ducked as the grandfather clock flew past us.

"That's better," I said, getting to my feet and wiping off the slobber as best I could. I turned round, ready to give the creature a piece of my mind. But when I saw it, I stopped. She was in tears, her tiny fluffy yellow paws covering her eyes.

"Er… Are you all right?" asked Max.

"No," she admitted.

Max gave me a look that said, 'Yeah, I know she just ate us and we have every right to be angry but she's clearly going through something right now, so we should probably be the bigger people and see if we can help her.' He packed a lot into that look.

I sighed. "What's your name?"

"Hungrabun." She sniffed.

"I'm Flo and this is Max," I said. "You want to tell us what's wrong?"

"What's wrong?" repeated Hungrabun. "Oh, just my life's dream being destroyed, that's all."

"Your dream was to eat us?" asked Max, understandably confused.

"What? No! My dream is to compete in the Battles but that's never going to happen. You were comfort snacks, and I can't even get that right. I'm such a failure."

I decided to skip past the part about us being comfort snacks. "The Battles? What are they?"

She looked up at us in shock, her eyes red from rubbing and snot dangling from her tiny nose. "You new in town?" she asked.

"Something like that," Max said.

"The Battles are a tournament where creatures team up and compete against each other," said Hungrabun, her face brightening as she explained. "Sixteen teams of two, each creature bringing their own unique abilities to the fight until only one team is left standing. I've been watching the Battles ever since I hatched. It's always been my dream to compete in them and now that I'm finally old enough it's not going to happen."

"Why not?" asked Max.

"Because I can't find anyone who wants to team up with me, and they don't let you enter as a single," she said. "You get overexcited and accidentally eat one or two potential teammates and suddenly word gets out and no one wants to be your partner. I coughed them both back up but no one ever mentions that part, do they?"

I grabbed Max by the arm and pulled him to one side. "I've just figured out what game this is," I whispered. "It's *Critter Clash*."

A look of realization dawned on Max's face. "Of course!"

Critter Clash was one of those games that everyone knew about, even people like Max who weren't into games. Playgrounds were always full of kids, or "creature coaches", discussing tactics or recounting glorious victories.

"I bet we have to help Hungrabun win the tournament to escape the game," I said.

Max nodded. "I think you're probably right."

"Help me?" sniffed Hungrabun. "But you don't look like creatures. You look more like … coaches. But no one's seen a coach in years."

"We are!" I said. "And we'd like to become yours."

"What does she mean no one's seen one in years?" asked Max.

"It's probably because *Critter Clash* is so popular they keep bringing out new versions," I whispered. "I got mine a couple of years ago but no one plays it any more and Mum won't let me get the new one because she says I've got enough games, which is ridiculous. How can anyone have enough games?"

"So what makes you qualified, exactly?" interrupted Hungrabun.

Max and I looked at each other. "Well, Max is really clever," I said. "He can come up with game plans and strategies and tactics, that kind of thing. And I can show you some awesome fighting moves."

"Oh yeah?" said Hungrabun. "Like what?"

"Like my Dropkick of Doom for starters," I said before launching myself into the air, feet first. Unfortunately I quickly discovered that doing the move while PLAYING a video game was a lot easier than doing the move while IN a video game. I landed on my back with a massive, embarrassing thud.

I looked up at Hungrabun, who didn't seem hugely impressed.

"Actually," said Max. "Flo is really good at making you do things you don't want to do."

I glared at him.

"But that's a good quality in a coach," he clarified, before adding under his breath, "Not always in a best friend, mind you…"

Hungrabun looked like she was giving the idea serious thought but then she just shrugged. "Even if I were to accept, weren't you listening earlier?" she asked. "The Battles are tag-team only. I can't enter without a partner. And the tournament starts tonight!"

"What if we could find you a partner before then?" I asked. "Could we be your coaches?"

Hungrabun gave us a long look before holding out her little paw. "Deal."

ABOUT THE AUTHOR

Tom Nicoll has been writing since he was in
school, where he enjoyed trying to fit in as much
silliness in his essays as he could possibly get away
with. When not writing, he enjoys playing video games
(especially the ones where he gets beaten by kids
half his age from all over the world). He is also a big
comedy, TV and movie nerd. Tom lives just outside
Edinburgh with his wife and two daughters.

LEVEL UP: BLOCK AND ROLL
is his tenth book for children.

ABOUT THE ILLUSTRATOR

ANJAN SARKAR first realized he loved illustration as a child when, with a few strokes of a crayon, he drew a silly face that made his mum laugh. Silly faces are funny and make people laugh, he thought. Since then, he's grown up into a hairy-faced man who draws silly faces for a living (not just for his mum). When he's not drawing he likes walking in the countryside and eating biscuits (sometimes he does both at the same time). Anjan lives in Sheffield with his wife and two kids.